Long Neck and Thunder Foot

HELEN PIERS Long Neck

and Thunder Foot

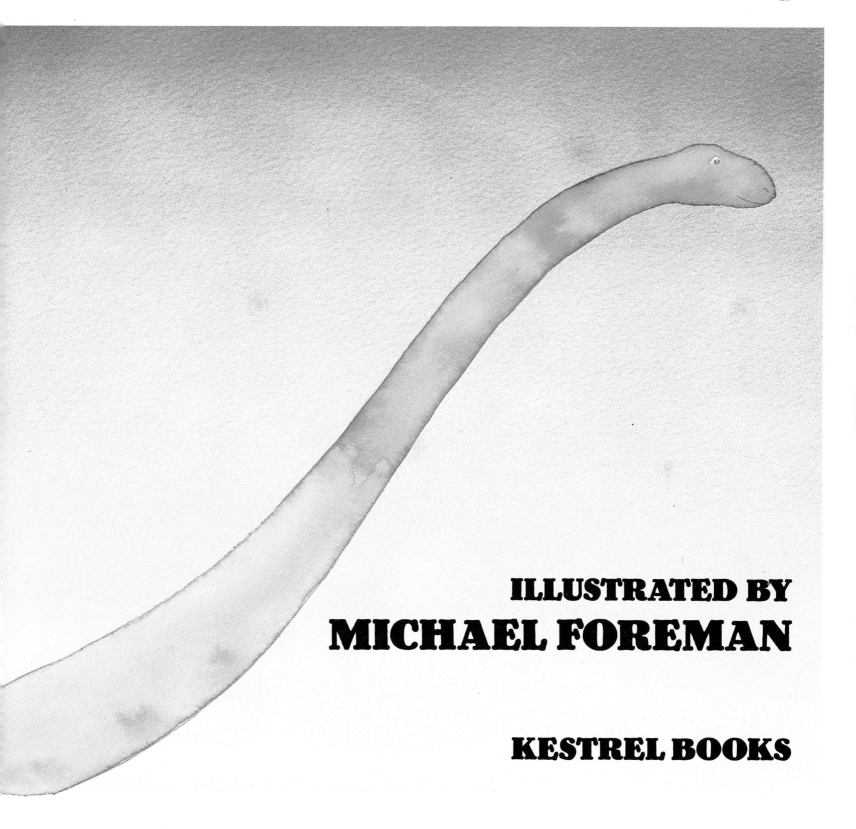

ILLUSTRATED BY
MICHAEL FOREMAN

KESTREL BOOKS

Long Neck the dinosaur lived alone in the forest.

   Apart from the birds and other small animals, Long Neck seemed to have the
whole world to himself. He could potter about all day, and at night he
could float on his back in the water watching the stars, and nobody bothered him.

One evening Long Neck was pottering about as usual, when he heard a noise like a clap of thunder. It came from close by. There were sounds of splashing too, and grunts and snorts. Long Neck trundled over to see what was going on.

There, splashing about in the swamp, was another dinosaur.
   Long Neck was very frightened – he had never seen another dinosaur before.
'He's so big!' Long Neck groaned.

The other dinosaur was Thunder Foot. Most of his time he spent digging in the mud for roots to eat, or chasing butterflies for fun.

Today Thunder Foot had chased a butterfly far from home.
Snorting and grunting, he was trying to keep up with it,
and every time he reached out to catch it he missed it,
and his feet banged together making a noise like
a clap of thunder.

Then Thunder Foot saw Long Neck staring at him.
Steam was coming out of Long Neck's nose, he was shaking
with fear, and his tail was thumping on the ground.
'Thump-dee-thump! Thump-dee-thump!'

But Thunder Foot, who'd never seen another dinosaur before, thought Long
Neck was shaking with anger.

'Heavens! It's a fierce monster, and he's thumping his tail at me threateningly.'

Now Thunder Foot began to shake with fear and the bony scales on his back
clapped and rattled together making a terrible din.

'He's making that rattling din just to frighten me!' Long Neck thought.
And his tail thumped harder than ever.

Long Neck and Thunder Foot began to circle around each other warily.
They would both have liked to turn their backs and run away; but they were
too frightened to do that.

'He might attack me when I wasn't looking,' they were both thinking.

The sun went down and the moon came out, and still the two dinosaurs
were facing each other, neither of them daring to take his eyes off the other for a
second. Then it began to rain. At last – just for a moment – Long Neck
took his eyes off Thunder Foot to watch a trickle of water running down his neck.

At once Thunder Foot leapt into the air and with head down and horns pointing forward . . . he turned and ran away.

At the same moment, Long Neck lifted his tail, and holding it high above his head, ran . . . in the opposite direction.

Later that night Long Neck was trying to sleep sitting up under a tree.
He couldn't float on his back in the water watching the stars as he usually did,
in case Thunder Foot came after him.

'Tomorrow I must do some strengthening exercises for my tail,' he was thinking.

Far away Thunder Foot was hiding under the water, but he kept his eyes
in the open air so that he could watch out for Long Neck.
  'Tomorrow I must sharpen up my horns,' he was thinking.

Next day Long Neck worked hard on his tail exercises, and, as his tail got stronger, he began to feel braver.

Thunder Foot sharpened his horns. When they were as sharp as two razors he began to feel more ready to meet Long Neck again.

Then they both decided to snoop around a bit – just to find out what the other was doing.

But when Long Neck saw Thunder Foot slicing up a tree with his terrible horns, he didn't feel brave any more.

And when Thunder Foot saw Long Neck send a tree toppling to the ground with one swipe of his tail, he crept away and hid.

'But I must do something, or he'll come and get me,' they each decided. And each of them made a crafty plan.

Soon Thunder Foot was digging a deep pit. He was pleased with *his* crafty plan. When he had finished digging, Thunder Foot trundled up the hill where he waited for Long Neck to come along.

'He'll fall in, and never be able to get out!' he grunted.

At the same time Long Neck hid in a tree with his tail trailing across the path below.

'He'll trip over it,' Long Neck thought. 'Then I'll give him a good swipe and get away quickly.' *He* was pleased with *his* crafty plan too!

Unfortunately, Thunder Foot didn't trip over Long Neck's tail. He sat on it instead. This was very painful for Long Neck.

He was trying hard not to howl with agony, when suddenly the branch on which he was lying gave up trying to carry twenty tons of dinosaur . . . !

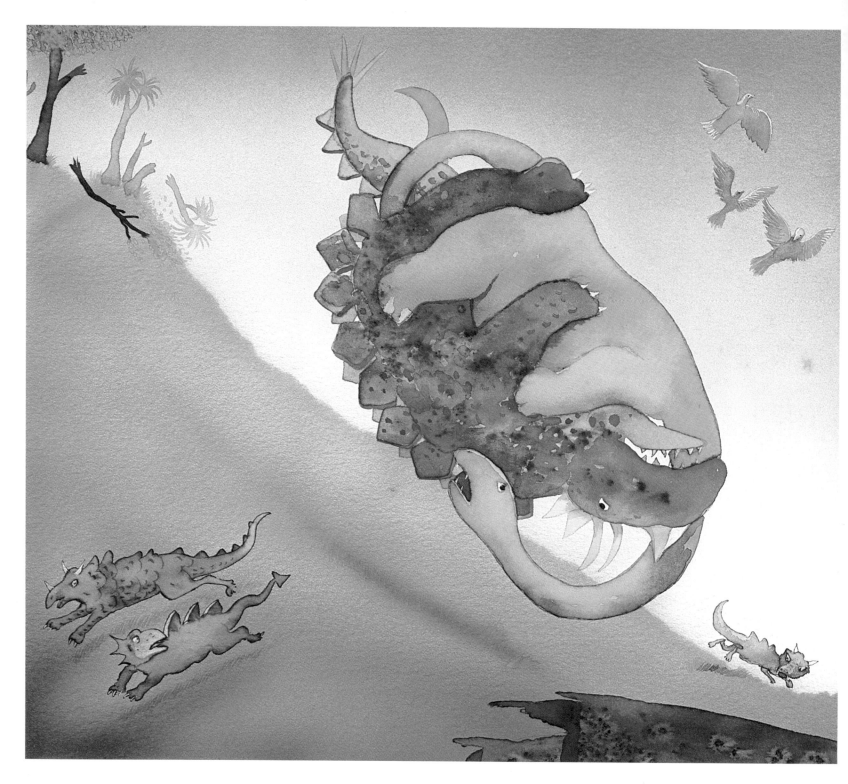

It was like an earthquake when Long Neck dropped on top of Thunder
Foot. The forest echoed and rumbled, and the whole world shook as they
rolled down the hill.

Then, at last, everything quietened down again.

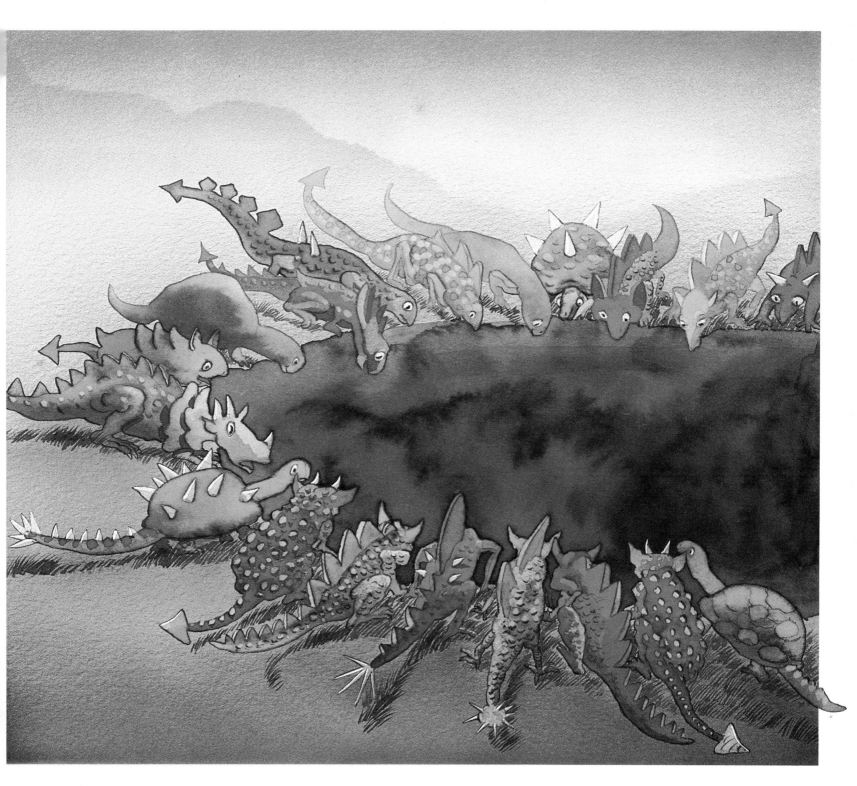

The only noises now were a kind of rattling din and a 'thump-thump-thump!' coming from Thunder Foot's deep pit. It was a long time before Long Neck heard Thunder Foot speak. His voice wasn't big and bellowing, as Long Neck had expected. It was a rasping *little* voice like his own.

'Are you going to eat me?' Thunder Foot was asking.

'I'm much too frightened to eat *anything* now,' Long Neck replied wheezily.
'Anyway, I'm a vegetarian.' Both dinosaurs were thinking hard now.

'It's not me you're frightened of, is it?' Thunder Foot asked at last.

'Of course it is!' sighed Long Neck. 'Are you frightened of me . . . perhaps?'
   'Very!' said Thunder Foot.
Long Neck's tail began to thump more slowly, and Thunder Foot rattled only
now and then and at last stopped altogether.

That evening Long Neck was floating comfortably on the water. He was very relieved, but he did feel he'd made a fool of himself.

'Never mind,' he thought. '*He* was as frightened as I was . . . I didn't know I could thump my tail like that. I wonder if I could do it again.'

Near by, Thunder Foot was snuggling under the water.

'But of course,' he was telling himself, '*he* was as big a coward
as me . . . I wonder if I could rattle like that even when I'm not afraid.'
   Next day he tried, and he could. Long Neck, too, found he could
thump his tail whenever he chose. And then they both had the same lovely,
crafty idea.

So it happened that not long after, on a clear starry night, the forest echoed with a loud rattling noise and the heavy 'thumpa-dee-dump-dumping' of a long tail beating out a rhythm on the ground.

Somewhere in the forest Long Neck and Thunder Foot were giving a party, and the birds and all the other animals of the forest had come out to sing and dance together to the beautiful music of the big friendly dinosaurs.

KESTREL BOOKS

Published by Penguin Books Ltd, Harmondsworth, Middlesex, England

Text copyright © 1982 by Helen Piers. Illustrations copyright © 1982 by Michael Foreman

First published in 1982. ISBN 0 7226 5704 8

Printed in Great Britain